Me Love Cookies

Read along as me tell you delicious story about cookies and other yummy foods. You will know it is time to turn page when you hear this sound.... Oh, me love that sound! Okay, here it is!

publications international, ltd.

1

Hello there. You hungry? Me hungry!

Me had nice breakfast, but that long time ago. What me going to eat now? Well, this may come as surprise, but me want...

COOKIES!

Me just reach into cookie jar and — WHAT? No cookies left? Uh-oh, me look in cupboard. No cookies. Me look on counter. No cookies. Me look under couch! Still no cookies!

Oh, me so sad. Oh, and me so hungry! Who ate last cookie?

4

Uh-oh. Me remember now. ME ate last cookie. Now cookies all gone.

Me cannot believe sun shining on day with no cookies! But no time to think about that. Me getting very, VERY hungry, and me have to eat something!

Me start to wonder. What other people eat when they run out of cookies? Tell you what me going to do. Me going to find out!

5

So, me decide it good day to try new foods. Yep, me head
out to Sesame Street where me cannot help but see Big Bird
appear to be eating something. Me waste no time wondering if it
cookie. Me ask politely: COOKIE!

It NOT cookie, Big Bird say. It snack of crunchy, yummy
sunflower seeds. He only have a few left, but he offer to share
them with me.

Me cannot say no to that.

SUNFLOWER SEEDS

Mmmmm. Yum. Me must admit sunflower seeds pretty good to munch on, but they all gone now and me still very, VERY hungry! Oh, how me wish to have big plate of COOKIES!

Oh look, there goes Elmo. Me wonder where Elmo going. Maybe he terribly hungry too, and looking for some cookies. Me decide to follow him. Bye-bye, Big Bird!

Oh! Oh! Me see Elmo at fruit stand getting banana. Usually me stick with cookies, but if banana good enough for Elmo, maybe it good enough for me.

Fruit stand lady very nice to monsters, and she have lot to say about fruit. She ask me, "Do you want a banana? I've got bananas. I've got strawberries and blueberries. And peaches too! Do you like oranges, apples, and grapes? What about mangos? I've got mangos!"

That one very excited fruit stand lady. Me tell her thank you for banana. It not cookie, but it very appetizing. So me try other fruit, too.

Me try ALL the fruit. That when fruit stand lady say maybe
Cookie Monster should try something else, like spaghetti.
She point across the street and tell me, "I sure do get hungry
for spaghetti looking at that restaurant across the way. I'd like
a yummy plate of spaghetti with tomato sauce and maybe
a meatball right on top!"

Me start to think, spaghetti sound delicious. Me ready
for spaghetti!

13

Oh boy, oh boy, oh boy. Spaghetti smell so good! (Oh, sorry, me forget you cannot smell in book. But me tell you, it smell almost as good as cookies.)

Waitress ask, "Hi there, mister. What can I get you?" Then me tell waitress me like to get big, heaping, gigantic — not to mention ENORMOUS — plate of spaghetti and meatballs, please. But me settle for one regular size plate.

Oh, me cannot wait. Mmmmm. Waitress say it coming right up. Hey, what that sound?

It fire truck siren! Next thing me know, plate of steaming spaghetti is plate of soggy spaghetti. Firefighter says everything okay, it just a mistake. No fire, that good, but no spaghetti, that very bad! Me extremely hungry!

Firefighter have advice for me. He say, "When I'm hungry, I eat something that's quick, in case I have to jump in my fire truck for an emergency." He tell me best food to eat on run is sandwich with big glass of milk.

It emergency RIGHT NOW. Me need sandwich quick!

Me figure deli counter good place to find sandwich. Maybe COOKIE sandwich?

Okay, okay, okay. So deli counter man does not recommend cookies in sandwich. That little disappointing. But turkey-lettuce-tomato sandwich turn out to be yummy!

Me finish up sandwich and think, per chance have cookies NOW, after sandwich? Me have been without cookies for so long. Oh, cookies, come to Cookie!

Uh-oh. Me get terrible news. Store has no more cookies! "I heard some monster bought them all yesterday," deli counter man say. "A big, BLUE monster."

What? All out of cookies? Oh, that VERY disappointing.

But me try to look on the bright side of things. While me here, me take opportunity to buy more sunflower seeds and fruit. Me even get spaghetti to make. And me take advice from deli counter man — who put together pretty tasty sandwich — and get some yogurt and carrots too.

21

Me almost cannot believe me got through whole day without cookies. Who would have thought me could do it?

Not me.

Do not get funny idea. Me Cookie Monster, and me LOVE cookies! Sure, new foods good. New foods tasty. New foods downright yummy. In fact, me pretty full from all the good stuff me eat today.

But me NEVER give up cookies!